THE TRAVELS OF
ATUNGA

THE TRAVELS OF ATUNGA

by

THEODORE CLYMER

Illustrated by

JOHN SCHOENHERR

An Atlantic Monthly Press Book
Little, Brown and Company
BOSTON   TORONTO

For Lois

who travels with me

FIRST EDITION

T 10/73

Library of Congress Cataloging in Publication Data

Clymer, Theodore.
    The travels of Atunga.

    SUMMARY: A young Eskimo seeks the help of two
powerful gods to bring food to his starving people.
    "An Atlantic Monthly Press book."
    [1. Eskimos—Legends] I. Schoenherr, John,
illus. II. Title.
PZ8.1.C595Tr   [E]   73-3158
    ISBN 0-316-14760-5

ATLANTIC—LITTLE, BROWN BOOKS
ARE PUBLISHED BY
LITTLE, BROWN AND COMPANY
IN ASSOCIATION WITH
THE ATLANTIC MONTHLY PRESS

Published simultaneously in Canada
by Little, Brown & Company (Canada) Limited

PRINTED IN THE UNITED STATES OF AMERICA

The old Eskimos tell of people and deeds of long ago; they speak of spirits, of magic and journeys like Atunga's.

These tales tell us much about how the Eskimo lives and the gods he fears and the ways he tries to please them. Sedna, the old woman of the sea, is the Eskimos' most powerful god. When she is pleased she sends seals, which provide meat, skins for warm clothing and oil for the lamps. Tungarsuq is lord of the land animals, a great god — but Sedna is stronger.

Atunga is not an experienced medicine man — an *angakoq*. Inexperienced but brave, Atunga must seek help from Tungarsuq and Sedna.

Even in the days before grandfathers, hunger was with the people.

Atunga decided he must visit Moon's land where deer and seals lived. His wife begged him to stay at home — but Atunga was strong in his wish to go.

One by one, Atunga darkened the lamps of his house.
He sat with his back to the lamps and asked his spirit
helper — his Tornaq — to take him to Moon.

Atunga waited.

His Tornaq did not move him.

Strong in his wish to visit Moon, Atunga made his way
to the Great Black Mountains where Tungarsuq, lord of
all the land animals, lives in a cave.

No one dares enter the cave.

Atunga called into the cave to ask Tungarsuq's help in getting to Moon. Atunga told of the people's hunger.

From deep in the cave came Tungarsuq's answer: "Go home, Atunga. Go back and ask your Tornaq for help once more. Tell him what I have said."

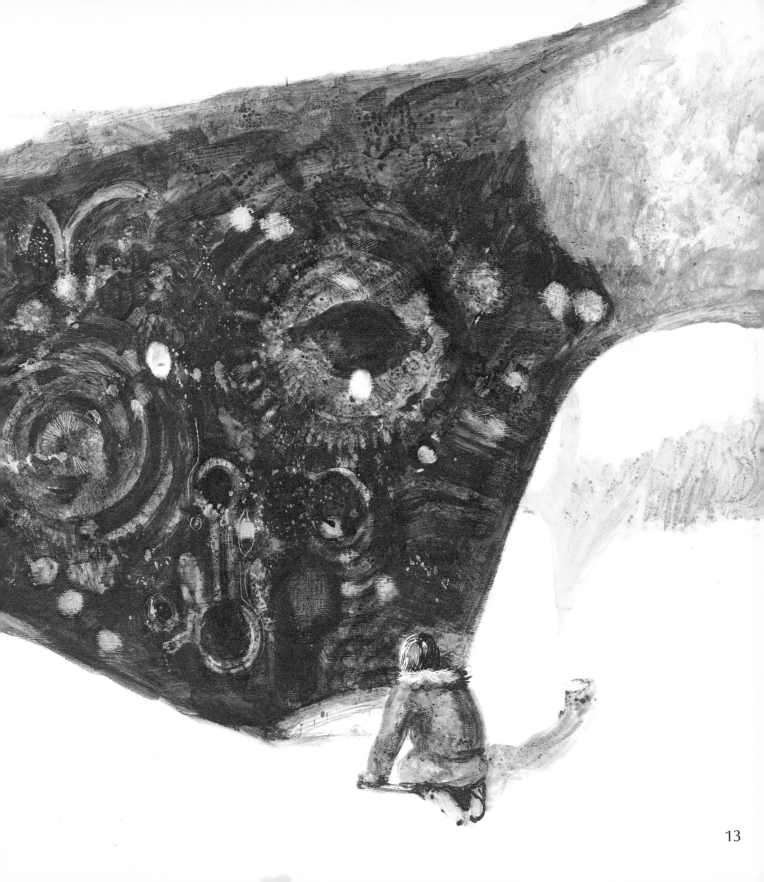

Again, Atunga sat in his house with his lamps darkened. Again he asked his Tornaq to take him to Moon. Atunga told of the people's hunger and his trip to the Great Black Mountains. He told what Tungarsuq had said.

Atunga waited.

His Tornaq moved him — but only a little.

Now Atunga wanted to see Moon more than ever. He went to find Sedna, the old woman who lives in the sea and is god of all the creatures of the water.

Atunga went to a rocky point and called for Sedna. She came up from the deep, dark water.

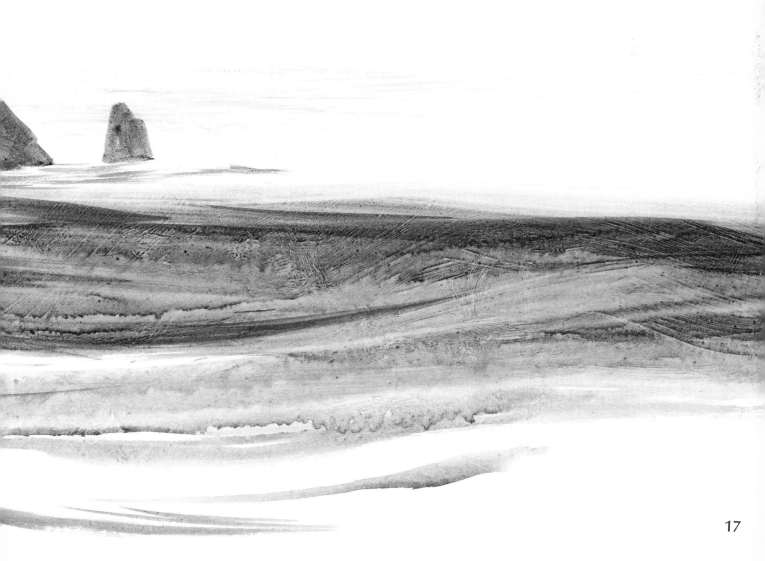

Atunga combed her hair and told her of his wish to visit Moon.

Sedna said, "Go home, Atunga. Go back and ask your Tornaq for help once more. Tell him I ask this."

Slowly, Sedna disappeared beneath the water.

19

For a third time, Atunga sat in his house. His lamps
were dark. He begged his Tornaq to take him to Moon.
He told of his visit with Sedna.

With his Tornaq's help, Atunga moved up into the sky. Then he walked on and on until he came to Moon's house.

Moon lives in a small house. White deerskins are always drying there. Moon sits in the first room. His wife, Sun, sits in the second room.

Deer meat was in Moon's land and in Moon's house, but none was offered to Atunga.

Sun and Moon did a strange dance while Atunga told Moon of the hunger of the people.

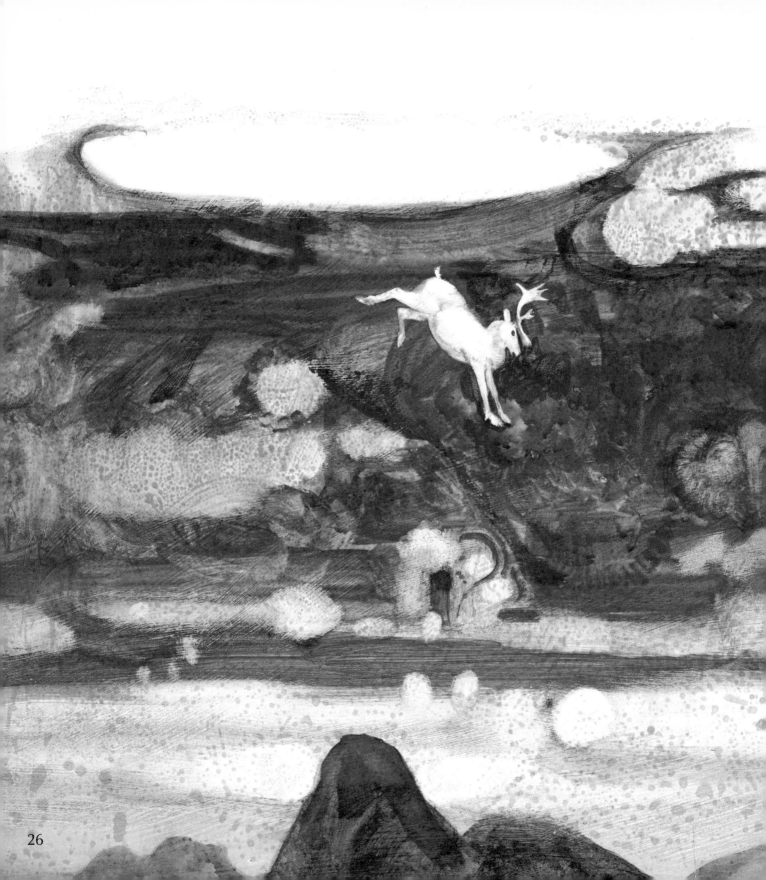

Then Moon led Atunga out of the house and let Atunga choose one animal from the land near Moon's house.

Atunga chose a deer and pushed it through a hole in Moon's land. The deer dropped to the Great Black Mountains near Tungarsuq's cave.

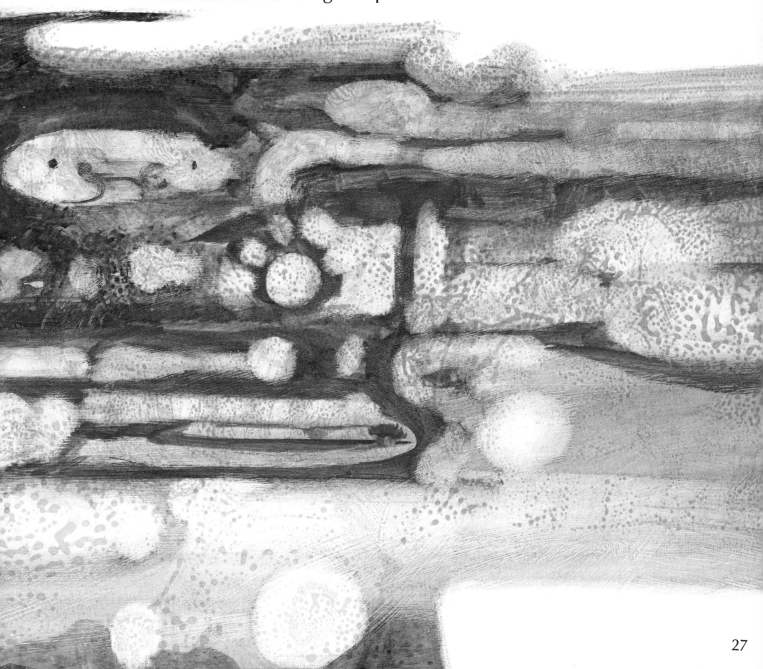

Moon let Atunga choose another animal. He took a
seal and pushed it through another hole. The seal fell
into the sea near the rocky point where Sedna lives.
Then Atunga went back to his own house.

30

Because of Atunga's visit to Moon, Tungarsuq now has deer to send the people. And from Sedna come the seals.

This story is true. The old men tell it.